FiZZY
STEALS THE SHOW

Michael Coleman

Illustrated by Philippe Dupasquier

ORCHARD BOOKS

ORCHARD BOOKS
96 Leonard Street, London EC2A 4RH
Orchard Books Australia
14 Mars Road, Lane Cove, NSW 2066
ISBN 1 85213 785 1 (hardback)
ISBN 1 85213 823 8 (paperback)
First published in Great Britain 1994
First paperback publication 1995
Text © Michael Coleman 1994
Illustrations © Philippe Dupasquier 1994
The right of Michael Coleman to be identified as the author
and Philippe Dupasquier as illustrator of this work has been
asserted by them in accordance with the
Copyright, Designs and Patents Act, 1988.
A CIP catalogue record for this book
is available from the British Library.
Printed in Great Britain by
The Guernsey Press Co. Ltd., Guernsey, Channel Islands

CONTENTS

by the same author

Fizzy Hits the Headlines

Redville Rockets
Fan-tastic Football Stories

1
Crash-Landing

"It'll never fly," said Maya.

Fizzy turned to her best friend. "Maya, believe me. This *will* fly."

"No," said Maya, "what I mean is, I don't think it will fly straight. The wings look a bit wonky."

Fizzy wrinkled her nose. Maya could be right. If she was honest, she'd have to admit that Maya usually *was right*.

7

"I think it will go round in a circle," added Maya.

"Well, I don't think it will fly at all," sneered the pigtailed girl sitting in front of them.

"Oh no?" said Fizzy. If there was one person in the class she didn't want to be right about anything it was Lucy Hardwick. "You wait until break. Then you'll see."

"Break?" said Lucy nastily. "Why not now? Mrs Grimm isn't here yet."

"But she soon will be ..." Fizzy started to say.

She didn't finish. With a cry of "Well I say try it now!" Lucy Hardwick snatched up the paper aeroplane from Fizzy's desk and sent it soaring into the air.

In the next few moments, both Maya and Fizzy were to be proved right.

Maya had said that the paper aeroplane wouldn't fly straight, and it didn't. Lucy Hardwick had sent it heading towards the front of the classroom, but it very quickly began to turn left ... and left ... and more left ... until it was shooting towards the classroom door. That was when Fizzy found

out she'd been right, too. Not about the aeroplane – but about Mrs Grimm, their teacher, turning up soon.

For, just as the aeroplane reached top speed and went into a dizzying dive-bomb, the classroom door opened and in stepped Mrs Grimm.

"Oh, no!" groaned Fizzy. The aeroplane was sticking out of Mrs Grimm's hair like a chocolate flake from an ice-cream cornet.

Fizzy closed her eyes and waited. She didn't have to wait long. In front of her, Mrs Grimm was already pulling the paper aeroplane from her hair and unfolding it.

One glance at the name written at the top, one glare around the room, and then … "Fiona Izzard!!! Come to the front this minute!"

Head down, Fizzy trudged to the front of the class for the sixth time that week. And it was still only Tuesday. "Yes, Mrs Grimm?"

Her teacher thrust the unfolded sheet of paper under her nose. "This landed in my hair!" she bellowed. "What is it meant to be?"

"A hair-o-plane ... I mean an aeroplane," said Fizzy.

"Wrong, Fiona! It is an important letter home to explain about our trip to the Millington Multi-Mart tomorrow. It is not meant to be an aeroplane! Made by you and thrown by you!"

"Made, yes," began Fizzy. "But ..."

"No buts!" yelled Mrs Grimm. "Now, go back to your place while I think about what to do with you."

Fizzy trudged back to her seat, past a sniggering Lucy Hardwick. By the time she was sitting down again, Mrs Grimm had produced a clip-board with a list of names on it.

"Now, class, as it says in the letter which I hope everybody else has still got ..."

"I have, Mrs Grimm," squeaked Lucy Hardwick.

"I'm sure *you* have, dear," said Mrs Grimm. "Now, as the letter says, I have

arranged with the Manager of the Millington Multi-Mart for us to spend tomorrow at
the store as part of this term's Community
Service project. The Multi-Mart, so the
Manager is always telling me, is the largest
superstore in the whole county. You can get
just about everything there."

"What will we be doing?" asked Lucy
Hardwick.

"Doing what comes naturally to you,
dear," said Mrs Grimm. "Being helpful."
She tapped a finger on her clip-board.

"Everybody has been given a job to do. Lucy, you will be showing customers where things are. If they don't know where to go, it's your job to tell them."

"I could tell Lucy Hardwick where to go," hissed Fizzy.

Next to her, Maya started to giggle. She stopped quickly, though, as Mrs Grimm said to her, "Maya Sharma, you will be on trolley duty. Your job is to help people push their shopping trolleys to the car park."

Mrs Grimm went on through her list, announcing jobs for everybody in the class. When she'd finished she looked round. "Now, have I missed anybody out?"

Slowly, Fizzy put her hand up. "Me, Mrs Grimm."

"Ah, Fiona. Of course. Well, I have a

special job for you. One entirely suited to your talents."

"Really?"

"Yes. Your talent for making a mess of things. You will be sweeping up. Instead of making a mess of things here, you can clear up a mess there."

17

2
On the Road

Fizzy leaned on her broom and sighed. "What's the time, Maya?" she asked, as her friend trundled by with an empty shopping trolley.

"Half-past ten."

"Is that all? It feels like midnight! It's all right for you trolley-pushers. You only have to go out to the car park and back. I've been round the whole store with this broom, you know. Grocery section, household section, toys section – even the tricks and jokes section."

"That bit must have been fun," said Maya, trying to cheer Fizzy up.

"No it wasn't," said Fizzy, "it was no joke at all. There were boxes all over the place." She pointed to the big pile in the corner. "And I had to clear them all up!"

"Mrs Grimm certainly doesn't seem to like you very much at the moment, does she?" said Maya.

"You can say that again," said Fizzy.

"Mrs Grimm certainly doesn't seem to like you ..."

"All right, all right!" said Fizzy. "Somehow I've got to get back into Mrs Grimm's good books. And do you know how?"

"No," said Maya. "How?"

"I don't know!" said Fizzy. "I was asking you!"

She looked glumly out towards the Multi-Mart's car park. For some reason a large crowd seemed to be gathering in the corner nearest the store. She edged a bit closer to the window.

"Hey, look at that," said Fizzy, beckoning Maya over.

Outside, a large lorry was arriving. It had the words "Radio Millington" splashed on its side and underneath them, in large flashy letters, "Ricky Rix's Road Show".

"Ricky Rix's Road Show," said Fizzy. "It must be coming from here today!"

As they watched, two men got out and started to open one of the lorry's panel sides.

"It is!" said Maya. "Look!"

The inside of the lorry had been turned into a small stage. Glitzy paper lined the

back and hung from the ceiling. Red and blue lights were flashing on and off. And there, slap-bang in the middle of it all, was a DJ's console: turntables, microphones, loud-speakers – the lot.

"Ricky Rix's Road Show," breathed Fizzy.

She had a strange gleam in her eye. "Hey, that could be it . . ."

"What could be it?" asked Maya, thinking that she probably shouldn't.

"The way to get back into Mrs Grimm's good books!"

"What? How? When?" Three questions in one go was a record even for Maya, but she was very confused.

"Ricky Rix's Road Show comes from a different place in Millington every week, doesn't it?"

"Ye-es."

"And he plays requests, doesn't he?"

"Ye-es."

"Asked for by people putting cards into his Win Bin . . ." Fizzy pointed as one of the men carried a large container to

the front of the stage. "And every person he plays a record for is sent a bunch of flowers!"

"Ye-es."

"So . . ." said Fizzy.

Maya got that sinking feeling. "So" was a word that usually spelt trouble where Fizzy was concerned. "Yeee-ees?"

"So, if Ricky Rix plays a request from me to Mrs Grimm, what will happen? She'll get a nice bunch of flowers and we'll be pals again! I mean, everybody likes to know they're thought a lot of, don't they?"

"But you don't think a lot of Mrs Grimm," said Maya.

"I do when she's not yelling at me," said Fizzy. "And if I can get a bunch of flowers for her she might not yell at me, so then I'd definitely think a lot of her. See?"

Before Maya could ask Fizzy to explain all that again, a booming voice came from the lorry. One of the assistants was standing at a microphone. Even from inside the store they could hear him clearly.

"One, two, three … testing … The Radio Millington Road Show, with the one and only Ricky Rix, will begin at 11 a.m. Put

your requests in the Win Bin at the front of the stage, if you please. Don't forget – 11 a.m. *Dooon't* miss it!"

Immediately people began surging forward to drop cards and pieces of paper into the Win Bin.

Fizzy looked around.

"The only problem is," she said, "what do I write my request on to make sure Ricky Rix notices it?"

Maya shook her head. "Wrong, Fizzy." She pointed to Mrs Grimm, who was standing on guard just inside the Multi-Mart's glass doors. "The problem is, how do you get past Mrs Grimm?"

Fizzy looked at the pile of boxes in the corner, then at Maya's shopping trolley, and her face broke into a broad smile. "Wrong,

Maya," she said, "the problems have all disappeared."

"They have?"

"Yep. I've just had a good idea. Correction, *two* good ideas!"

3

Trouble in Store

Fizzy held up the large card, cut from one of the cardboard boxes. "One request!"

"Ricky Rix won't be able to miss that," admitted Maya. With Fizzy's message on one side, and a picture of a top-hatted magician on the other, it was certainly a card that stood out.

"Right!" said Fizzy. "And if he can't miss it, he's bound to pick it!"

She looked out towards the doors. Mrs Grimm, arms folded, was still on guard. "Now all we've got to do is get it to him."

Maya started to push her empty trolley away. "Well, I'll be seeing you later ..."

"Hold on," said Fizzy, "I need you!"

"Oh no," said Maya firmly. "Not me. I'm a trolley pusher."

"I know," said Fizzy. "That's why I need you!" She began to load boxes from her pile into Maya's trolley. "All you've got to do is what Mrs Grimm has asked you to do – push this lot of boxes out to the car park."

"And where are you going to be?" asked Maya.

Fizzy beamed. "That's my second good idea." She began to climb into the trolley.

"I'm going to be where nobody can see me. Underneath the boxes!"

Mrs Grimm had positioned herself next to a large pyramid of drinks cans which had been set up just inside the Multi-Mart's glass doors.

Peeping out from the side of the trolley Fizzy saw that they were getting closer to them. She burrowed a bit deeper beneath the boxes. It was a great plan. Nobody could possibly see her. It was going to work!

Suddenly, the trolley stopped.

"Hello, Maya." It was Lucy Hardwick.

"This is ever such an interesting store," Lucy was saying. "I just showed a customer to the tricks and jokes section."

The tricks and jokes section? Fizzy's heart sank. If Lucy Hardwick had seen her climb into her hiding place . . .

"Oh, yes. They've got everything there, you know."

"Have they?" said Maya. Mrs Grimm was looking their way. She began to edge the trolley forward.

"Oh, yes. Everything. Like this stuff."

Fizzy heard a rustle, followed by a rip. Lucy had taken a paper sachet from her pocket and torn it open.

"What stuff?" she heard Maya ask.

Lucy laughed one of her nastiest, sneakiest laughs. "Sneezing powder, Maya! I wonder if it works on boxes?"

The next thing Fizzy knew, a cloud of grey powder was cascading through the gaps in the boxes and down on top of her. Immediately she felt her nose begin to twitch. If she sneezed now, so close to the doors, Mrs Grimm would be bound to spot her.

"Get a move on, Maya!" she hissed. "Before I . . . aah-aah . . ."

As the trolley moved forward again, Fizzy put a finger under her nose. It didn't help for long. They drew level with the pyramid of drinks cans and another cloud of powder was shaken down on top of her.

"Aaah-aaah . . ." Not much longer. Fizzy held her nose as tightly as she could.

"Aaaah-aaaah . . ." They were past the pyramid and level with Mrs Grimm. Fizzy heard the doors swish open. If she could only hold on for two more seconds . . .

She couldn't. Like an exploding balloon, Fizzy let rip with the loudest sneeze she'd ever sneezed in her life.

"Aaaah-chooooooooooo!"

Suddenly everything went haywire.

As she sneezed, Fizzy's arms and legs flew upwards of their own accord, sending the empty boxes shooting into the air. Almost at once, somebody screamed. "Oh! Oh! Get it off!"

Fizzy turned round. The screaming was coming from Mrs Grimm. One of the boxes had landed on her head, like a cardboard hat that was ten sizes too big.

"Get it off, I say!" yelled Mrs Grimm. "I can't see where I'm going!"

And she couldn't, either – which is why, with her arms stretched out in front of her, Mrs Grimm walked straight into the pyramid of drinks cans.

The pyramid began to sway.

First it went one way. Then the other.

Suddenly Lucy Hardwick scampered over to it.

"Lucy, help!" yelled Fizzy. "If that lot falls over I'm in real trouble!"

"Really?" said Lucy. And with that she stretched out her hand towards the tottering pyramid – and took a can from the middle.

Clang! Bong! Clonk! Gdong!

The whole pyramid collapsed in an explosion of noise.

"Now what do we do?" screamed Maya.

Through the chaos, Fizzy saw the answer at once. Mrs Grimm still had the box on her head. Their teacher couldn't see where she was going. And if she couldn't see where she was going -- then she couldn't see them!

So ... if they were out of sight when she took the box off ...

"Giddy-up, Maya!" she yelled. "Run!"

Maya ran. She ran out through the swishing doors.

Out into the car park. And straight through a gap in the crowd surrounding Ricky Rix's Road Show.

4
Air Mail

"Intro-ducing! The one ... and the only ... Ricky... RIX!"

From the depths of the shopping trolley Fizzy couldn't see what was happening, but she could guess.

Ricky Rix, with his giant spectacles and giant smile, would be striding on to the makeshift stage. He would be taking up his position behind the DJ's console. Any

moment now, he would be introducing the Road Show to all the Radio Millington listeners.

"Good morning, Millington!"

"Good morning, Ricky!" shouted the crowd.

It sounded as though there were lots of people around them. Fizzy popped her head out of the trolley. "Where are we, Maya?" she asked. "Are we close to the front?"

"No," said Maya. "I don't think we're even close to close to the front."

Ricky Rix's voice boomed out over the loudspeakers once more. "Okay, okay, okay. Time to hit the Road Show, everybody! Bring me the Win Bin!"

Fizzy stood up in the shopping trolley. At the side of the stage one of the assistants was lifting the Win Bin with its pile of requests inside.

"We're going to be too late," cried Fizzy. "We've got to get to the front!"

Maya shook her head. "We can't. Look at the crowd."

Fizzy looked. All around them people were standing shoulder to shoulder.

"We'd have to bulldoze our way through," said Maya.

"Or go between their legs," groaned Fizzy.

"Or fly," said Maya.

Fizzy's eyes opened wide. "Fly?" she said. "Fly?" Suddenly she started scrabbling in the trolley for her request card. "Maya, you're a genius!"

She hopped to the ground and laid the card in front of her. She bent down and began to fold it. Once, twice. Then again. Until ...

"An aeroplane?" said Maya. "You don't mean ..."

"Never heard of air mail?" laughed Fizzy.

"But ..."

Fizzy wasn't taking any notice. She'd jumped back into the shopping trolley and was standing on tip-toe.

Up ahead, the Win Bin was now at Ricky Rix's side. "Here we go!" he shouted into the microphone. "It's request time. Every card I choose means a big, beautiful, super-smelleroony bunch of flowers for some-body."

"Stand by for blast-off!" yelled Fizzy.

"But ..." tried Maya.

"No buts, Maya, as Mrs Grimm would say. This is my last chance."

With a cry of "There she goes!" Fizzy

RADICAL SILI

launched her aeroplane into the air.

Only then, as it hurtled off towards the distant figure of Ricky Rix, did she turn back to Maya and ask, "So, what were you going to say?"

"I was going to say," said Maya, "that one of the wings wasn't straight – again."

Fizzy looked at Maya, then up at the soaring aeroplane. "You mean ..."

Maya nodded. "I think it's going to go round in a circle – again."

And she was right – again.

Fizzy's flying request card was already starting to veer off course. Instead of heading for the stage it was now heading for the driver's seat of the Radio Millington van. Suddenly a gust of wind caught it.

Up into the air went the card, still turning.

Then it started to come down.

Down and down, it came.

Past Ricky Rix.

Past the radio van.

Past the crowds of people.

And straight through an open office window in the Millington Multi-Mart.

5
Fizzy Calling

Fizzy watched it disappear. "Well, that's that. My last chance to get into Mrs Grimm's good books." She shrugged. "Still, I suppose things could be worse."

"They could?" said Maya. She glanced anxiously over Fizzy's shoulder.

"Course they could. I mean, Mrs Grimm could have taken that box off her bonce and spotted me, couldn't she?"

"Er ... yes."

"And she could have seen us come over this way, couldn't she?"

"Fizzy ..."

"I mean, Mrs Grimm could be standing behind me right now, couldn't she? So things could be worse, couldn't they?"

Fizzy felt a heavy hand on her shoulder. And heard a voice she knew all too well.

"Fiona Izzard," growled Mrs Grimm. "I *am* standing behind you right now. And, believe me, as far as you are concerned, things couldn't possibly get any worse!"

By the time Fizzy had put the can pyramid back together again, the Road Show was just about over.

"That's it, folks," boomed Ricky Rix as the final request faded out. "See you again next week. Same time, different place!"

"Unlike your work for the rest of the day, Fiona," said Mrs Grimm, "which will be in the same place. You will sweep the whole of the Multi-Mart. And when you have fin-ished – you will sweep it again!"

She thrust the broom back into Fizzy's hands and pointed towards the grubbiest corner of the store. "Off you go. And don't forget, I will be close behind you."

But no sooner had Fizzy started sweeping than an announcement crackled out over the store's tannoy system. "Would Lucy Hardwick and Fiona Izzard please report to the Manager's office. Lucy Hardwick and Fiona Izzard."

"Through that door, dear," said Mrs Grimm as Lucy came scampering across. A soft look came into her eyes. "And up the stairs. That's where he works."

Fizzy followed Lucy Hardwick through a door marked "Private". "Maybe they're giving a prize for today's best helper," said Lucy, as they went up the short flight of stairs, "and I'm going to get it."

"Oh, yes?" said Fizzy, "what about me?"

"After your day, I expect you're going to get it too," crowed Lucy. "In the neck!"

They were met at the top of the stairs by an unsmiling man in a blue suit. He introduced himself as the Manager, then led them along a corridor to a room at the end.

"Sit there, please," said the Manager to Fizzy, pointing to a chair.

Fizzy sat where she'd been told to – and stared. The Manager's office had an enormous window which stretched the length of one wall. And through that window she could look down on everything that was happening in the Multi-Mart.

She could see people pouring in from the car park now that the Road Show had finished. And, right underneath the window, she could see Mrs Grimm and the rest of the class staring up at her.

"Attention please, Ladies and Gentlemen."

Fizzy looked round. The Manager was holding a microphone and speaking into it. Of course, she realised, this must be where they made announcements from – bargain offers and that sort of thing.

"This is the Manager speaking. Please stand by for a very important announcement."

Everybody turned to stare up at the office. Fizzy felt like a goldfish in a bowl.

"And here to make that announcement is – Miss Fiona Izzard!"

"Her?" squeaked Lucy Hardwick. "What about me?"

"Ah," said the Manager. "You are going to be a TV personality."

"I am? Ooh!"

"Oh, yes. Earlier on today our security camera showed you taking some sneezing powder without paying for it, not to mention a can of drink which caused a major display to collapse. We will be watching that film later in the company of your teacher. As for now, though ..." He turned back to Fizzy. "I would like you to make that announcement."

"Er ... what announcement, exactly?" said Fizzy. Surely she wasn't going to have to apologise to the whole world over the Multi-Mart's tannoy system?

No, she wasn't. The Manager was smiling. What was more, he was holding out something that Fizzy recognised – her aeroplane!

"It landed slap-bang in the middle of my

desk," he said, handing the aeroplane back to her. "So, why don't you read out the message on it and see what happens."

"Me? What? Where?"

The Manager pointed to a microphone on the desk Fizzy was sitting at. "Through that," he said. "Go on."

Fizzy turned to the microphone. She gave a cough, and started to read what she'd written earlier.

"Dear Ricky Rix. Can you please send a big bunch of your best flowers ..."

"... bunch of your best flowers ..."

Fizzy heard her words echo around the store. Funny, she thought. She hadn't noticed the Manager's voice echo.

"... to my teacher, Mrs Grimm ..."

"... to my teacher, Mrs Grimm ..."

An echo there definitely was, though. Fizzy looked out through the glass. Down below, Mrs Grimm and the rest of her class were impressed, she could see that. They were all staring up at her, open-mouthed.

"Most of all, can you tell Mrs Grimm I don't mean to get on her nerves ..."

"... get on her nerves ..." echoed the echo.

"And I'd like us to be friends."

"... like us to be friends ..."

"Thanks a lot ..."

"Thanks a lot ..." went the echo.

"Signed," read Fizzy, "Fiona Izzard."

"Otherwise known as Fizzy," went the echo, this time with a laugh.

With a laugh? Since when could echoes laugh? Or make up their own words?

Fizzy swung round – and saw how. Behind her, holding the Manager's microphone and a massive bunch of flowers was – Ricky Rix!

"I owed the Manager a favour for letting the Road Show use the store's car park," said Ricky.

"And," said the Manager, "when your card arrived on my desk I couldn't think of a better favour to ask."

"So," said Ricky, "shall we go and deliver these flowers? And ask Mrs Grimm if the whole class can come to the Radio Millington studios for a visit next week?"

"Wha ..." It was Fizzy's turn to stare open-mouthed. She didn't do it for long, though. "You bet!" she yelled.

She looked out of the window. Down below, Mrs Grimm was doing something Fizzy couldn't remember ever having seen her do before. She was smiling – at her!

Somebody shouted, "Fizzy's on air!"

And they were right. Fizzy left the Manager's office feeling as though she *was* walking on air.

She didn't look back as the Manager closed the door to his office with a huge smile.

Had she done so, she would have seen the sign on his door. And then she would have discovered why he was almost as pleased as she was at the way things had turned out.